WINGATE FOOTBALL CLUB

A story by
CLIVE SINCLAIR

GW00745995

ROLLING BALL PRESS

First published in *Hearts of Gold*,
Allison & Busby, 1979
Reprinted in *For Good or Evil: Collected Stories*,
Penguin 1991 and
Contemporary Jewish Writing in Britain and Ireland,
Peter Halban, 1999

This edition published by
Rolling Ball Press, 16 Canonbury Grove
London N1 2HR
in association with the Menard Press

Copyright © Clive Sinclair 2013

ISBN 978 0 9926 868 0 2

Edition limited to 500 copies,
numbered and signed by the
author, of which this is

No. 236

Preface

I can't say exactly when my father first took me to see Wingate play, but the earliest programme I have is dated 1957. On its front is a cartoon by David Langdon (later ones feature the work of Nero, as Harry Blacker signed himself). It also carries the autograph of Ted Kid Lewis, said to have been (by Mike Tyson, no less) 'probably the greatest fighter ever to have come out of Britain'. As it happens his grandson is my son's agent in LA. Who needs an old school tie when you have Wingate FC in your CV?

My father must have recognised Ted Kid Lewis, and asked him to sign the programme. He knew about boxing. When he was a boy his family (in those days the Smolenskys) shared their house with the Finns, who trained champions. Presumably Ted Kid Lewis was the guest of Al Phillips, whose brother Ray was one of Wingate's finest. Al Phillips was hardly less of a boxer than Ted Kid Lewis. Fighting as the Aldgate Tiger, and sporting a Mogen David the size of the Ritz on his shorts, he had punched his way to the Flyweight Championship of Great Britain. In his prime he was ranked as No 3 in the world.

He is the original of Al Pinsky in the story. The fracas in which he participated occurred much as I described it. I cannot remember the name of the boy who precipitated the fisticuffs, but Wingate's opponents were Cray Wanderers. Wingate certainly won the cup that day, but I cannot now be sure that I have provided an accurate record of the match.

Solomon, the story's tragic hero, is invented, but there was a boy in my year at Orange Hill named Solomons, who had some phobia concerning rugby balls, and was forced by our sports master to overcome it by grasping a ball and running head-first at a line-up of Amelekites. It was the same sports master who made the remarks about Jews and games recorded in the story. Take a bow Mr Beaky White. I no longer recall the size of his eponymous nose, but it must have had semitic pretensions to earn for him such a soubriquet.

In 1957 the Sinclairs (my father changed his name when he got his call-up papers) lived at 352 Watford Way. Hall Lane, where Wingate played, was a five-minute walk away, on the other side of the A41, then a modest two-lane blacktop. At the junction of Hall Lane and the Watford Way was a large Express Dairy depot and stables, whence our milkman would emerge every morning with his miniature stagecoach like some pasturised John Wayne.

Everyone knew my father at the ground. Why not? He was, after all, chairman of the Supporters' Club. We purchased our programmes, which always contained an advertisement for his company, Simbros, manufacturers of furniture in distant Islington (a few minutes' walk from where I now live), and our raffle tickets (which we never won once, in all those years) and took our places on the touchline among our fellow Jews.

The Arabs may have had Lawrence, but we had his distant cousin, Orde Wingate, who inspired Israel's armed forces, and, more indirectly, the football club that won my heart. Unfortunately Wingate did not win very much else, leading the editor of the programme to note one week: 'We know that our desire is to make friends on the field of sport, but not by presenting our opponents with two points!'

He was referring to the club's motto: *Amicitia per ludis*. Being the 'only Jewish club in the country playing senior league football', Wingate was founded to demonstrate that Jews could be Corinthians – Spartans even – as well as victims. Of course no one believed that stuff about friendship through sport; respect is what we really wanted: the respect of others, but above all, self-respect. We knew that our opponents weren't Nazis, but the fact that they were *goyim* and we were Jews gave the games their edge. We identified not with the rabbis on the *bima* in Rayleigh Close or Danescroft synagogues (I, for one, accompanied my father on Saturday mornings, and sniffed sawdust and glue instead of snuff and ancient prayerbooks) but with the *minyan* plus one on the pitch.

As the tension mounted and the clock ticked down to 4.40 on those long-ago afternoons, men around me lit their Woodbines or their Players and the air became suffused with the smoky perfume of smouldering tobacco. To this day I cannot smell cigarette smoke al fresco without being transported back, Proust-like, to Hall Lane and the Promised Land of my childhood.

Hall Lane is still extant, but all else has changed. The Watford Way is now uncrossable. Wingate Football Club has moved to Finchley, and changed its identity. Wingate's former ground has been transformed into a housing estate. The settlers who live there now do not know it, but their dwellings stand upon a field of dreams.

The story opens with an hypothesis: if England were to play Israel in the World Cup, which team would the narrator support? Back in the 1970s, when the story was written, it seemed an impossibility. But in 2007 the two nations played each other twice, being in the same qualifying group for the European Championship. The first match, in Tel Aviv, was a nil-nil draw; the second, at Wembley, took place on September 8, a Saturday. Israel played as if the rabbis had given them permission to turn up, but not to actually touch the ball. They lost three-nil. And I sat by the waters of Babylon, and I wept.

September 2013

Wingate Football Club

There are some dilemmas it is better not even to think about. I'll give you a for-instance. Suppose England were to play Israel in the World Cup. Whom should I support? Ah, you will say, such a thing is very unlikely. England's football is stale, Israel's half-baked. But I'll tell you, stranger things have happened, like when Wingate won the London League Cup.

When I was a boy I used to go with my father to watch Wingate play on Saturday afternoons. Wingate were the only Jewish team in the entire football league; named in honour of our version of Lawrence, crazy Orde, a *goyisher* Zionist. Wingate were never a great team, and though they always had a couple of good players they usually spent the season near the bottom. So imagine our astonishment when we won a hard tie away from home and found ourselves in the London League Cup Final.

Our opponents were a dockland team, notorious for their anti-semitic supporters. They came to our ground like a wolf on the fold. But that year we had a brilliant outside-right, in real life a ladies' hairdresser. To me his dizzy runs down the wing were a thing of infinite beauty; left-backs tumbled to the ground when he passed, felled as if by magic. Pursued by these humbled clods he sprinted for the corner flag and unleashed acute crosses that sent their goalkeeper flailing in the air. Our centre-forward leapt and dived fearlessly to meet the winger's passes, but each time he missed by a hair's breadth.

'Only connect!' we yelled in encouragement.

The supporters of our opponents were prepared to tolerate our precocious start; content in the knowledge that Jews lacked spunk they waited for the crunching tackles to crush the life out of our challenge. And then our centre-forward did connect; his head met the pass fifteen yards out. The ball had 'goal' written all over it as it shot like a bullet towards the net. The goalkeeper was frozen, as helpless as a rabbit, but – would you believe it? – even as we were celebrating, the ball hit the post and rebounded back into the centre of the field. We cheered, nevertheless. But my father said sadly, 'A miss is as good as a mile.' And in my disappointment I felt the full force of the simile: all that marvellous approach-work had been for nothing because finally the ball had missed, the nearness of the miss didn't enter into it, a miss is as good as a mile.

A minute later I learnt another lesson. The rebound initiated an enemy attack which petered out harmlessly in the midfield mud, but then our centre-half made a disastrous error; although unchallenged he passed back to the goalkeeper, and to our horror the ball again stuck in the mud. It was a race for the ball between our goalie and their centre-forward, an ox. The goalie was first to the ball but before he could fully grasp it the centre-forward had crashed into him, not illegally but carried by the momentum of his run. The ball spun from our goalkeeper's hands and bounced into the back of the net. We protested, hurled abuse at the referee, but the goal stood.

'Take note of that, young man,' said the Prince of Shmattes, who sported a velvet-collared camel-hair overcoat. 'It is an important lesson to learn: that the end justifies the means. We Jews have always been too fussy. When did pussyfooting around ever get us anywhere? Why can't our forwards barge into goalkeepers like that? Look at me. Did I make a success by tapping on doors? Not on your life. No, I barged straight in. Believe me, that's the only way to get on in this life.'

Now that we were losing, the other side's supporters even cheered our outside-right and mocked their own left-back for being made to look foolish by the quicksilver jewboy.

The second half started with a sensation. Straight from the kick-off the ball went to our outside-right who rounded his man with arrogant ease and set off on one of his runs. At the last possible moment he crossed the ball and our centre-forward rose like there were springs in his heels to meet that perfect pass. He seemed to be floating while the ball rested on his instep before he smashed it into the back of the net. The equaliser! We went delirious with joy, we felt the exultation that perfection excites; make no mistake, that goal was a work of art!

We breathed the ultimate in praise, 'The goalie never stood a chance.'

But try as they might our boys just could not get that second all-important goal. Then ten minutes from time our right-half, laughingly overweight but astute with it, split their defence with a through ball which left our centre-forward alone with only the goalkeeper to beat.

'Shoot!' we pleaded.

He ran on, seemed to stumble, but kept his footing.

'Shoot!' we screamed.

But he hesitated. What was in his mind? Was he planning to dribble round the goalkeeper? However, before he had a chance to do a thing the goalkeeper suddenly rushed from his line and knocked him flat. The referee pointed to the spot. A penalty! Grown men, including my father, hid their faces as the centre-forward prepared to take the kick. This time there was no hesitation, before the tension had time to sink in the ball was in the goal. We could hardly believe it; less than ten minutes to go and we were ahead; we began to scent victory.

'WIN-GATE! WIN-GATE!' we chanted.

'How much longer?' I kept asking my father as the final minutes ticked away and the tension became unbearable. The attacks of our opponents grew increasingly desperate; their centre-forward charged again and again into our defence like a battering-ram. But our defence held. What a relief when the referee looked at his watch and put the whistle to his lips!

As the whistle blew a woman in a fake leopard-skin coat said out loud, 'Hitler was right! Send the Jews to the showers!'

The boy standing next to her was one of our supporters (he looked big to me, but I don't suppose he was older than fourteen).

'Keep quiet, you bitch!' he said.

Whereupon she slapped him round the face. He hit her back.

'You dirty Jew!' she cried.

Her companion moved in on the boy, but he never hit him more than once before Al Pinsky interceded. Now Al wasn't tall, so that *golem* just laughed, which was daft, because Al Pinsky was once the lightweight champion of Great Britain. The *golem* dropped the boy and took a swing at Pinsky. His fists were the size of hams. Pinsky ducked, like he was taking a bow, then straightened up and calmly knocked the fellow cold. When the police came and listened to the various versions of the incident we tingled with the pleasure of righteous indignation. That evening as I walked home with my father towards the awaiting glass of milk and toasted challah I felt elated; we had not only won the cup but also a great moral victory over the *yoks*. They had called us dirty Jews and we had stood up to them and got away scot free; on the contrary, it was they who left with bloody noses.

Now I realise that part of the fun of going to Wingate was the possibility of encountering just such anti-semitism. Among our supporters it was axiomatic that if you scratch a *goy* you'll find an anti-semite: our world-weary version of Shylock's great lament. Perhaps we had the mentality of people who go to the zoo to tease a caged lion and complain when it tries to bite them; but I think we welcomed the anti-semitism because it proved that we were morally superior; it may have confirmed our status as outcasts but it also reaffirmed our role as the chosen people. Although our daily existence gave us no evidence to support the fact, there obviously was *something* different about us. And on Saturday afternoons we could flaunt this difference with pride, knowing that it would be recognised; we were the Wingate Supporters Club; our badge was the Mogen David. On the field our boys gave as good as they got, and on the sidelines if the *yoks* wanted trouble they could have it from us wholesale.

A couple of weeks after we won the cup, as if to rub in our moral superiority, the *Daily Mirror* ran an exposé of the horse-doping racket, and it turned out that most of the opposing team and many of their supporters were involved, including their centre-forward and the *shiksa* in the leopard-skin coat. That Saturday we were full of the news; it was too good to be true, not only were they anti-semites they were criminals as well!

'What else can you expect from *yoks* like that?' said the Prince of Shmattes.

My father, a wittier man, said, '*Goys* will be *goys.*'

Of course my ambition was to play for Wingate. Every evening after school I would go into our back garden and chase a football around. I divided myself into two imaginary teams: the first mounted dazzling attacks down the flank which were finished off by a deadly striker, and if a goal was not perfect they would not count it; the other was made up of plodders, grateful for any rebound or accidental goal they were without grace and had no time for the brilliant individual. The first team did not necessarily win, but they were always a pleasure to watch. As I ran I daydreamed of being the prince of outside-rights: the outsider who hovers on the periphery of the match but whose brilliant interventions win the day. What better ambition for a Jewish boy?

Our games master at school had flaming red hair and a beak of a nose, though he wasn't Jewish. Since my natural expression was one of dis-comfort I was his constant butt.

'Stop looking like you are suffering,' he would say. 'Boys are supposed to enjoy games.'

My passion for football came as a surprise to him; in fact I was fleet-footed enough to be a good outside-right.

'Not bad,' he said, 'I didn't think your people liked physical activity.' He took a look at my expensive football boots and said, 'I bet your father earns a lot of money, eh?'

'I don't know,' I said.

I hadn't been going to watch Wingate for nothing; I knew an anti-semite when I saw one.

Because I enjoyed football I was spared actual physical torment. However, my friend Solomon was a different kettle of fish. Solomon hated all games, especially football.

Poor Solomon was a coward, and Beaky sensed this at once. He picked out the six biggest louts in our class and told them to stand in a line. Then he threw the ball to Solomon and ordered him to run at them. Solomon didn't move. He was too scared even to argue.

'Get going you milksop, or else,' said Beaky.

Still no action from Solomon. So Beaky hit him, hard, round the head. 'You have no choice, you greasy tub of chopped liver,' said Beaky.

Milchik or *flayshig*, it made no difference to him. Solomon ran at the boys in the line, kicking the ball far ahead of him, but not one of the boys bothered to go for the ball, taking their cue from their master they took Solomon instead. While Beaky watched they beat him up; not badly, but enough to make him cry. I make no excuses for my inactivity, I was only glad it wasn't happening to me. Besides, it was a part of our games lesson.

About the time I went away to university things began to go wrong for Wingate; lacking enough Jewish boys to make a *minyan* they had to co-opt non-Jewish players. It was true that Wingate was supposed to foster good-fellowship between Jewish and non-Jewish footballers, but most of our supporters felt this was going too far; this was – bite your tongue – assimilation. Gradually they stopped coming to watch Wingate and sure enough, as they had prophesied, the club lost its identity. The last time I saw them play the team was made up of strangers, men with names like Smith and Williams. The old atmosphere was gone. Wingate had become just another football team. At university I would continue to listen to the football results on the radio, but I could never feel for any other team what I had felt for Wingate; that sense of personal involvement was gone for ever. But by then I knew that there was more to life than football.

My parents assumed I had gone to university to get a degree, but I really went to lose my virginity. I became educated as a by-product. I discovered that the seminars were the great showplaces. So I made myself shine. Society functions were another good place to meet girls. I picked up Linda at the Jewish & Israel Society. Linda called herself the most experienced virgin in the western hemisphere; she would allow any physical intimacy short of intercourse. We slept together frequently, and sometimes I would get such a belly-ache from frustration that I could hardly stand up straight. In public we acted like lovers, but we were just going through the motions, like footballers without a ball. Still, thanks to Linda, I learned all about the role of the kibbutz in Israeli life. Not to mention the role of the Arab, the artist, the woman, the socialist and the *frum* Jew. One night a real Israeli came to speak. I had never seen a *sabra* before. He was swarthier than I expected. His subject was the role of peace in Israeli life. He was optimistic. He pointed out that it was now over a decade since Suez, and while there was no de jure peace there was clearly a de facto modus vivendi. A policy of live and let live. He believed that the Arabs had come to accept the presence of Israel, and that given time a normal relationship would develop between the former enemies. Had he got the wrong number!

When the Six-Day War began we didn't know that it was only going to last six days, of course. What trauma there was in the diaspora! No one gave Israel a chance. Every night we saw a different Arab army on the news. Their leaders promised to drive the Jews into the sea. Then Abba Eban would appear, sounding like a Cambridge don. The words of the Prince of Shmattes came back to me. 'We Jews have always been too fussy. When did pussyfooting around ever get us anywhere?' Even Solomon's mother knew better than Abba Eban what was what.

'The Israelis should give the Arabs a bomb already,' she said; 'they should only suffer one hundredth of what we Jews have been through.' She looked about ready to *plotz*.

No wonder, her son was in the Israeli army. After school, instead of going to university, Solomon had emigrated. We still kept in touch. He had a room in Jerusalem. Till the war-fever got me this had been my only real contact with Israel. But now it was time to separate the Jews from the *goys*. Of course I couldn't enlist in the Israeli army but I volunteered to go out as a driver of tractors or – God forbid – ambulances. I was warned that I might come under fire, but I brushed aside the possibility. However, my services were never required. The war ended too quickly.

It made for excellent television. Don't forget, it was my first war; I was too young to remember Suez. Every night I went to the television room next to the library to watch the late news. It was marvellous, our side were winning victory after victory. Films showed tanks scooting over the Sinai Desert; the enemy were nowhere in sight. Soldiers hugged and kissed beneath the Western Wall of liberated Jerusalem, looking like they had just scored the winning goal. Experts explained with the aid of mobile diagrams the brilliance of the Israeli strategy: the daring raids, the lightning strikes. I had not felt such exultation since Wingate took the London League Cup; but I was older and I savoured my triumph in silence. Linda, beside me, was less circumspect. She screamed, she cried. I told her to shush, because we were not alone. Sitting by himself, the only other person in the room, was an Arab. Night by night his expression became progressively gloomier. When, on the seventh day news came in of the Syrian atrocities, the captured Israeli pilot decapitated in front of the cameras and worse, he got up and walked out. 'What do you expect from Arabs?' said Linda.

Solomon's mother telephoned, *shepping naches*; her song was 'my son the hero'. His next letter was modest enough, but it made me envious. Of all people, Solomon had become glamorous! An outside-right, as it were. Such madness, to feel deprived because I had missed a war! But both Linda and I were engulfed in the exuberant aftermath. We discussed the possibility of marriage. We planned to become Israeli citizens. My Jewish destiny was about to be fulfilled.

Or so I thought. But chance took control: I was offered a post at the university – too good an opportunity to be missed. My destiny was postponed. Many other things also happened: governments fell, El Fatah became fashionable, Germany were revenged upon England in the Mexico World Cup, my parents celebrated their silver wedding, Linda and I were married.

We went to Israel for our honeymoon. Naturally we visited Solomon in Jerusalem. He was no longer the weedy Yid of our schooldays; instead he moved through the city with self-confident ease. A man among men, a real Yiddisher *mensh*.

One night after a street-corner supper of felafel we all went to the cinema in Zion Square. The first feature was a film about the Six-Day War, made up cheaply from bits of old newsreel. It was received with wild enthusiasm. Though it is difficult to credit today the audience cheered every time Moshe Dayan or Yitzhak Rabin appeared on the screen. Unfortunately the main feature was less to the crowd's liking: the story of a man destroyed by Stalinism, fiction based on fact. The audience quickly lost interest, and only perked up when the unlucky victim was accused of being a Zionist.

Finally, as the man looked through his prison bars towards the sky, someone shouted, 'He's expecting the Israeli air force to come and rescue him!'

Everybody laughed. As we were leaving Linda, unable to restrain herself, started yelling at a bunch of the yahoos. 'What is the matter with you,' she cried, 'don't you have any respect for suffering?'

'*Ma zeh?*' they said, tapping their foreheads.

Then Linda, out of control, spat in their faces.

This caused them to forget their good humour; they swore at Linda, they called her a whore. They gathered their empty Coca-Cola bottles and flung them at us; and as the glass shattered on the concrete floor they began to close in. Four Esaus, looking for a fight. What sort of joke is this, I thought, to be beaten up in Israel by fellow Jews? With a single movement Solomon grabbed the leader, clutched him and positioned him; then with a graceful gesture cast him over his shoulder. The unsuspecting partner of this *pas de deux* performed a somersault in the air and crashed on to the floor. His hairy brethren rushed Solomon, but it was a half-hearted attack, and Solomon danced amongst them till they all fell dizzily to the ground, like the walls of Jericho.

'Where did you learn to fight like that?' I asked.

'In the army,' said Solomon. 'I was the lightweight wrestling champion.'

He invited us to feel his biceps.

'You know what,' he said, 'whenever I fight someone I still imagine I'm hitting Beaky, that anti-semitic bastard.'

'But they were Jews you beat up tonight, Solomon,' I said.

'Only Yemenite Jews,' he said, 'it's all they understand.'

So even in a nation of Jews there were still *yoks*. Next thing we heard about Solomon was that he'd been chosen to represent Israel at the Munich Olympics. Quite an achievement for Solomon, the boy who hated games. We watched the opening ceremony on Solomon's mother's colour television; you should have seen her *kvell* as her only son marched past behind the Israeli flag. I'll swear her chest swelled out a good six inches. Poor woman, it was her last bit of pleasure.

Solomon did moderately well in his competition, though he did not win a medal; but he had his day of fame, none the less. He was probably sleeping when the Black September terrorists burst into the Israeli athletes' quarters. All through that day we sat in front of the television set seeing nothing but those white walls and the gunmen on the balcony in the balaclava helmets, hearing nothing but banalities from sports commentators unaccustomed to dealing with such events. We knew that Solomon was inside. What could he be thinking? Deeper than the politics of the Middle East, was he tormented by a single thought? That Beaky was having the last laugh. Solomon could not wrestle with men holding machine-guns; his skills were trumped, he was as helpless as a schoolboy again. When darkness fell we saw the coaches fill, ready to take the terrorists and their hostages to the airfield outside Munich. Linda swore that she could make out the features of Solomon, but all their faces looked the same to me. Written on them all was the awful realisation that whatever they did the Jews were doomed to lose out; you learn to fight to defend yourself against the *yoks* and – what happens? – they get guns and shoot you instead. One of the athletes looked back on the steps of the coach – perhaps that was Solomon – and held out his hands as if to say, what more can we do? Then at midnight came the surprise news. There had been a shoot-out at the airfield. All the hostages were safe. The terrorists were dead.

'Thank God for that,' said Linda.

The *Daily Mirror* was sticking through our letter-box next morning, like a dagger in a corpse. The headline screamed: THE TRAGIC BLUNDER. It seemed that the German police had made a 'tragic blunder' in announcing the result of the shoot-out; they got it the wrong way round: it was the athletes who were wiped out, not the terrorists. I began to shiver as the information sank in. Solomon was dead! I recalled with what pride he showed us his biceps that night in Jerusalem; but all the training was gone for nothing now. Solomon was dead. Linda cried all day, she cursed the Palestinians. But I could not see it like that, to me the Palestinians were instruments of fate, Solomon's inevitable nemesis; it was merely a cruel irony that this particular death struggle should be between two semitic peoples.

Out of habit I turned to the sports section of the newspaper. But what I saw turned me cold. 'Queens Park Rangers went hurtling out of the League Cup,' I read, 'following two tragic blunders by Rangers defender Ian Evans.' It had been quite a night for tragic blunders! The carelessness of some sub-editor had equated the two events, the terrible with the trivial; or perhaps it did really reflect how others saw the Munich Massacre. As a good away win for the Palestinians. It was, indeed, confirmation of Beaky's final triumph.

All this happened a few years ago, already. Since then the news has not been too good: nothing seems to have gone right since the Yom Kippur War. They have even built a mosque in Regents Park. Last week I met the Prince of Shmattes in the street. Only he isn't so clever any more. These days he has to wear his own *shmattes*. People stopped buying his suits and the economic crisis finished him off. He was on his way to the post office to collect his pension. Solomon's mother never recovered from the shock, and was senile before she was sixty. Now every young man who visits she thinks is her son, me included. And I go along with the pretence. What harm in that? My parents keep nagging me to give them a grandchild. But I want any child of mine to be born in Israel. *L'shanah haba-ah birushalayim.* Next year in Jerusalem.